# CHRIS

## River Valley Lawmen Series

### Book One

## CHERYL WRIGHT

Contents:

# CHRIS

## RIVER VALLEY LAWMEN SERIES
### Book One

Copyright ©2018 by Cheryl Wright

Cover Artist: <u>Black Widow Books</u>

# Thanks

Thanks to my very dear friends (and authors), Margaret Tanner and Susan Horsnell for their enduring encouragement and friendship.

Thanks also to Alan, my husband of over 45 years, who has been a relentless supporter of my writing for many years.

And last, but by no means least, thank you to all my wonderful readers who encourage me to continue writing these stories. It is such a joy to me knowing so many of you enjoy reading my stories. I love writing them as much as you love reading them.

# Chapter One

**Charlotte Jones shifted** in her seat.

It had been a long drive from Los Angeles to River Valley, Montana where her aunt lived.

She'd packed her whole life into the little trailer she was pulling behind her beat up Honda, but it had to be done.

She'd sold off what could be sold, given away what she no longer wanted or couldn't bear to see, and the rest, what little of it there was, she bundled up to take with her.

It was all she had left of her five-year marriage to Dale Jones. Along with regrets.

Five years of absolute bliss. Of being married to the man she held most dear in her heart.

He was the best husband, best lover, and would have been a fantastic father.

They'd had plans. Big plans. About their marriage, about their future, and about their future family.

Kids. Lots of them. They were going to sell their tiny two-bedroom apartment in Los Angeles and look for a big house out of town.

Where there was land. Somewhere for their yet to be conceived kids to run around and play and enjoy the outdoors.

Their house would be double storey, and their children would run up and down those stairs despite being told not to. They might even try to slide down the banister.

It would be huge, with at least five bedrooms, perhaps even six. There would be a playroom for the children, and the kitchen would be massive. It would need to be with that many kids.

They would plant a vegetable garden, buy some chickens, perhaps even have a cow to milk.

They had it all worked out. Dale was working his way up the ladder of the LAPD and was planning on taking his sergeant's exam soon. He desperately wanted to achieve that before applying for a transfer.

Charlotte's catering business, albeit in the early stages, was bringing in money, nearly but not quite enough to earn a full-time living. But ever the supportive husband, Dale didn't care. He just wanted her to be happy.

They had it all worked out. With the money Charlotte was earning, and with his raise for being a sergeant, along with the money from the sale of their apartment, they'd have almost enough to buy their dream home.

First though, they had to reach their goals.

Then find the perfect house.

Their forever home for their four plus kids.

Charlotte's heart began to beat faster. She wiped sweat from her forehead and wriggled about in the driver's seat. Her thoughts about the past were making her uncomfortable, and she fought back tears.

She pulled to the side of the road and let the tears fall until they became heart wrenching sobs. It was time, she decided, having shed virtually no tears until now.

She tried to chase the memories away with her tears, but they were steadfast in their endeavour.

She recalled that moment three years ago with clarity. It was still ever so vivid in her mind. Etched into her memory forever, almost like an old movie she replayed over and over again.

The moment she opened the door to Dale's distraught sergeant, she knew something was very wrong. When she noticed two fellow officers, close friends of Dale's standing behind him, faces white as a sheet, it was confirmed in her mind.

Her husband and soulmate was dead.

~~~

Deputy Chris Dolan let the cool air wash over him as he lay in bed.
~~~

The night had been hot, and he'd tossed and turned for most of it, wishing it would end. Now that it had, he felt like he needed another hour or two of sleep.

It wouldn't happen.

He sighed.

*Coffee.* He needed coffee.

Desperately.

He pulled on his jeans, leaving them open for the moment, and headed for the kitchen.

Then remembered the coffee machine had died. He'd grab one at the sheriff's office.

Feeling a little agitated over the broken coffee machine, he was tempted to skip his shave this morning. But he caved and headed for the bathroom.

When that arduous task was done, he jumped in the shower, letting the warm water wash over and down his aching body. Wresting the bad guy to the ground tended to cause those sorts of problems. It didn't happen ten years ago. He was a little younger, and a lot more fit back then.

He turned off the hot water and let the cold water roll over him. For about five seconds. What was he thinking?

At least he was more awake now than he was ten minutes ago. He groaned. *Was he really? He desperately needed coffee!*

Pondering the day ahead of him, Chris smiled. He never knew just what his day held in store for him.

It could be peaceful and serene one minute, then all hell could break loose.

He sure did love his job.

~~~

Chris strolled into work, coffee still on his mind.

The longer he didn't have it, the more he felt like a bear with a sore head.

"Morning," he grumbled under his breath as he walked past the reception desk. "Need coffee," he said, heading for the break room.

"Broken."

He heard the words trailing behind him as he continued walking, then suddenly stopped. "Broken? You've got to be kidding me." He ran his hands across his chin. He really did need coffee to give him a jump start in the morning. "Are you certain?"

The receptionist didn't get the chance to answer.

"Definitely broken," Sheriff Chase Callahan confirmed, coming out of his office. "But I think we have some granulated coffee somewhere."

Chris pulled a face.

"Don't tell me. You haven't had your coffee this morning," Chase said. He grinned broadly. "We're going to have a wonderful day," he said, chuckling as he turned to walk away.
~~~

"My machine at home is broken too. Must be the day for it," Chris told him. "Gotta have coffee. If there's nothing pressing, I'll whip over to Aunt Lizzie's and grab a cup." He started to walk away, then spun back to face Chase.

"You? You're worse than me in the mornings." Now it was Chris's turn to chuckle.

"Sure, thanks." Chase shoved some notes into Chris's hand. "Grab tucker too. On me today." He grinned, then went back into his office.

Chris wondered what was up. Not that he was a scrooge, but it was not like Chase to be shouting coffee, let alone 'tucker' as Chase had called it.

It got his interest up.

~~~

# The deputy strolled into Aunt Lizzie's

Kitchen, the local café, and glanced about as the little bell above the door tinkled.

The place was near empty, which wasn't unusual for that hour of the day. Not that Chris went there often, because he didn't. He'd be lucky to buy a coffee once a month. But since his machine was busted, that could prove to change.

Aunt Lizzie was standing behind the counter, cleaning the benches, and preparing for the mid-morning rush.

"Deputy," she said, nodding at him.

He tipped his hat. "Aunt Lizzie. How are you today?" He couldn't see anything out of place, yet he
~~~

knew something was amiss. It just wasn't like Chase to hand over money like that.

"What can I do for you, young fella?" Everyone was young to Aunt Lizzie. Even those who were over thirty, like him.

"Coffee for two – to go," he said. "And a bite to eat. It's for Chase and me," he added. Being locals, he didn't need to tell Lizzie how they had their coffee. She was amazing; she knew every person's name and how they had their beverage of choice. Cappuccino, latte, hot chocolate, whatever, she knew it by heart. Even whether they had regular, skim, almond or soy milk.

He wasn't sure what the town's people would do if Lizzie ever decided to sell the business. He shook his head. That would never happen. At least he hoped it wouldn't; everyone loved the woman standing before him.

Lizzie stood silently and thought for a moment. "We have some new items on the menu – freshly baked apple cinnamon muffins," she said. "Or there's apple slice, lemon meringue pie, or…."

She was interrupted with noise from the kitchen.

A young woman was carrying a tray of muffins. The smell coming out of the kitchen was divine and had his taste buds working overtime.

"Ah, here are the apple cinnamon muffins now." Chris turned toward the kitchen to see a complete stranger.

He stood watching for about thirty seconds, then tipped his hat to her, eventually pulling it off his head.

She stood tall, her long brown hair tied back in a pony tail. The same flour that was sprinkled across her face also covered the black apron tied around her waist.

"Ma'am," he said after long moments of unintentional staring, feeling more than a little curious about the newcomer.

"Let me help with that," he said, suddenly rushing toward the young woman, and offering to take the tray.

His hands reached out, and their fingers touched. Their eyes met momentarily.

"I'm fine," she said. Then she smiled. "But thanks."

He took a step back and straightened up. Lizzie stood to the side, watching the interaction and grinning.

"What?" he demanded, when he noticed her out the corner of his eye.

She was covering her mouth with her hand, but it was too late. He'd already seen the twinkle in her eye. "Oh, nothing," she said, obviously quite amused about something.

The tray was deposited on the back counter, ready for the muffins to be placed in the glass display case once they cooled down.

"Christian," Lizzie said. "This is my niece, Charlotte Jones."

He winced inwardly. Lizzie always insisted on using his full name instead of shortening it like everyone else. She was the only one that did. "Pleased to meet you, Ma'am," he said, stretching across the counter to finally shake her hand. "But everyone calls me Chris. Your aunt is the only one who calls me Christian."

"Nice to meet you too, Christian," Charlotte said with a smile, then looked across at the older woman who had a big grin on her face.

Lizzie knew he didn't like to be called Christian, but she insisted. She really loved to stir him up.

"Coffee's ready," Lizzie told him, still looking amused. "Did you want the muffins, or something else?"

"The muffins, I guess," he said, still wondering about Charlotte.

"You'll love them," Lizzie said. "Charlotte made them. It's going to be wonderful having her around."

She pulled her niece close and gave her a hug. "Charlotte has agreed to help me out," she added. "It was starting to get too much for me."

*Too much? For Aunt Lizzie? Since when?*

His interest was suddenly even more piqued. "Oh? Are you holidaying here?" he asked, turning to the newcomer.

She looked to her aunt before answering. "River Valley is my new home. Sorry, I have to get back to the kitchen," she said before scurrying off.

"Tell Chase I said he needs to cut down on the coffee," Lizzie said, gazing into his eyes.

Chris stared back. "What do you mean?" He was confused.

Lizzie looked at him and laughed. "He's already been in this morning. Met Charlotte too," she said, still chuckling as she bagged the two muffins.

Chris paid, then reluctantly left. He wanted to find out more about Chase's earlier visit. It was fairly obvious Chase had set him up.

Chris wasn't interested in a relationship. Any relationship. After what happened to his brother.....

A shiver shot through him.

He didn't want to think about it.

~~~

**Sheriff Callahan was** sitting at his desk doing paperwork when the deputy arrived back in the office.

He tapped on the open door, then shuffled inside. "Lizzie wondered if you're drinking too much of this," Chris said blandly as he handed over the hot coffee and still warm muffin.

Chase chuckled and took a sip of the scalding beverage. "Did she indeed?" He grinned at Chris, obviously not embarrassed he'd been caught out.
~~~

Chris took a long draw of the revered liquid and savoured it, rolling it around in his mouth before swallowing. "Oh my God. I really needed that," he said as he leaned back in the comfortable chair.

Opening the paper bag, he pulled a piece off the muffin and shoved it in his mouth. "Oh my Lord. That is divine!" Lizzie was a fantastic cook, but this outdid anything she had ever made. "How long is Charlotte helping Lizzie, do you know? These are to die for."

Chase finished what was in his mouth before answering. "Totally agree. Amazing, absolutely amazing." He stuffed more muffin in his mouth. "No idea how long she's helping out. Lizzie didn't say," he said once his mouth was empty again. "But she did say she's living here now, so we can only hope."

"Mmmmm, these have been sent from heaven." Chris took another huge sip of coffee, then went to stand.

"Stay," Chase told him. "We have stuff to go over. Besides," he said, grinning as he did. "I want to hear all about Charlotte. Was she nice?" Chris glanced up at him. He didn't appear one bit guilty. He wouldn't be surprised if Chase and Lizzie planned this between them.

She was renowned for setting up the town's bachelors with young women. Who's to say she wouldn't do it for her own niece?

"You ought to know," he said, getting annoyed. "Since you met her already. Don't you go setting me up. You and Lizzie are good at that sort of stuff." He gulped down the last of his coffee and snatched up his muffin as his pager went off.

It was going to be a long day, he was certain.

~~~

**Charlotte put another** batch of muffins in the oven.

This sure was a busy store her aunt had. She'd had no idea Aunt Lizzie's Kitchen was so busy. She'd have moved here sooner if she realised how much her aunt needed her help.

Lizzie had been pleading with Charlotte for over a year, but she'd thought it was just to get her away from the tragedy that had struck. To help distance herself from the memories.

She'd denied it all along, and now Charlotte could see first hand that Lizzie had been telling the truth and not just trying to help her out.

Her dear Aunt Lizzie really did need assistance.

While not an old woman, Lizzie was not young either. Charlotte wasn't sure exactly how old she was, but she had to be at least in her 50's going by the age of her own mother, who had died some years ago after being struck by a car as she walked across the road.

She didn't dare ask Lizzie's age - that would not go down well!

She cleaned down the kitchen counter, ready to make the next batch of whatever was needed. She
~~~

stuck her head out the kitchen door to see how busy the store was and was amazed.

Nearly every table was taken up, and there was a queue almost out the door. Her aunt had told her it got busy mid-morning, but she certainly didn't expect this. Especially with River Valley being such a small town.

But her idea of a small town, and Aunt Lizzie's were apparently two totally different things.

Two young women scurried about, one taking orders, and the other serving the customers at the tables. Lizzie manned the coffee machine. The part-timers only came in during the busiest of times.

How Lizzie had managed mostly by herself was a puzzle Charlotte knew she'd never solve. It was obviously taking its toll on her aunt, as she seemed to be moving slower than she'd ever seen before.

"A product of getting old," Lizzie had told her, but Charlotte wasn't so sure. More a product of doing too much, she was certain.

All of that would change as of right now.

She ventured out into the main area of the store and stood behind the counter assessing what baked goods needed replenishing.

With two batches of muffins in the oven nearly ready to come out, it looked like she should make some more apple slice and perhaps even lemon meringue tarts. They were both very popular.

As she headed back to the kitchen an idea popped into her head. Aunt Lizzie had never sold cake by the slice. That could be quite popular, especially for those eating in.

She decided to make a carrot cake, a black forrest cake, and a cheesecake. They'd always been popular when she'd catered for parties and weddings back home.

On second thought, she'd just go for carrot cake and see how that sold, then reassess. The mid-morning rush was almost over, so she didn't want to go into overkill.

She pulled all her ingredients out and started to prepare the cake batter.

She was enjoying having free-reign in the kitchen. It was her domain now, Lizzie had told her.

It was so wonderful living here. Being with her aunt and being able to help her out. Not just for the sake of it, but for her aunt's sanity and health.

And she was certainly enjoying the peace and quiet of country living.

She sighed. *Why didn't she move here sooner?*

Of course she knew the answer to that question; she was afraid she'd leave behind all memories of Dale. Of her wonderful husband and everything that went with that. Friends, police support, and the unit they'd lived in together for so long.

But that would never happen. How could she ever forget the love of her life? The heart of her very being?

She'd never forget him, and she knew it.

Charlotte swiped at an errant tear and took a deep breath. She needed to stop thinking and start working.

The timer went off on the oven and she pulled the next batch of apple and cinnamon muffins out and placed them on a tray to cool. So far they were her most popular item. What would the customers think when she introduced some new baked goods?

It had been a hard slog training as a pastry chef. She was working full-time, then going off to school at night. Dale knew it was her dream to open her own catering business and encouraged her.

Even when it meant they didn't get to spend quality time together. He still pushed her to finish her course, so she could follow through on a life-long dream.

And she did. But at what cost? They lost so many precious hours together.

*How was she to know he would be gone from her life so soon?*

Charlotte closed her eyes and braced her shoulders. Why did these thoughts come to her at the most inopportune times?

*Why did her darling Dale have to die?*

Lizzie came rushing through the door, flustering about. "We're out of muffins!" she said, then noticed them on the cooling racks. "Oh thank goodness."

She looked across at Charlotte. "Are you okay, sweetie?" Her voice was soft, as though she knew what

Charlotte was going through. And of course, she did, as her own husband had also died young. In much the same way as Charlotte's darling Dale.

"I'm fine," Charlotte said, reaching for the tray. "I'll bring them out in a moment."

Lizzie stared at the ingredients that had been rounded up. "What are you making?" she asked curiously.

Charlotte glanced up from what she was doing. "Carrot cake," she said. "I thought it might be a nice change for your customers."

Lizzie clapped her hands together. "That will be wonderful," she said excitedly. "The lunch crowd will love it!" She grabbed the tray of warm muffins and left the kitchen with an added spring in her step.

Moments later she popped her head back into the kitchen. "By the way, they are *our* customers now." Quick as a flash, she was gone again.

Charlotte pondered Lizzie's last words. She hadn't even thought about how long she would stay in River Valley.

In her mind, this was an extended vacation, but she certainly loved the place so far.

She hadn't met many of the locals yet, as she'd spent most of her time where she loved it most – in the kitchen.

She smiled.

This was what she always wanted to do. But the smile soon left her face. If only Dale had been here to see how far she'd come.

She braced her shoulders and got back to her carrot cake batter. It wouldn't be long before the lunch crowd were looking for something to eat. And she needed to ensure there was plenty of variety to choose from.

~~~

**Before Chris even got** out the door of Chase's office, the sheriff's pager also went off.

Something was going on.

Chris lifted his eyes to look at Chase, who was staring at him. It sounded serious and all available police were required to attend a hostage situation in a nearby town.

Chris took a deep breath. In all the years he'd been a deputy, he could only recall one other time when the River Valley police had ever been requested to attend a situation outside their jurisdiction.

That one had ended well. He wasn't so sure this one would, given the information they had so far.

Chase turned toward the safe and removed his gun. It was rare for any of the uniformed members to carry their firearms in the building. It wasn't necessary.

Chris scurried off to his office to do the same.

They met at the sheriff's car a short time later. "I'll coordinate everyone while you drive," Chase instructed.
~~~

And that's exactly what happened. As Chris drove, lights and sirens blaring, Chase organized the rest of the uniformed members.

It wasn't long before they heard the sirens of the other officers not far behind them.

"There." Chase spotted the scene before Chris did, and indicated where he should pull in. He parked not far behind a police vehicle from another county, and they gingerly moved forward, hands on their guns.

Chase went over and spoke to the hostage negotiator, then walked back to Chris and the rest of his team. "Sit tight and wait," was all he said. "So far it seems to be under control."

So they did. They stood around watching and waiting. For the next three hours. It was quiet. Too quiet, Chris felt, but they stayed put as they'd been asked to do.

"He's coming out." It was the negotiator. He'd managed to convince the perpetrator to let his girlfriend and their three-year-old child go. But he was willing to give himself up first.

Praise the Lord.

The front door opened, and two officers ran toward the perpetrator. He wasn't very old, late 20's Chris guessed. But he was agitated. Very agitated.

Chris didn't like it at all. He was prepared to move quickly if necessary, and he was sure it would be.

As the two officers got closer, the man turned back and reached for something inside the door. He was so quick no one realized what was happening before a shot rang out.

It was at that point the scene turned into utter and absolute chaos. At least ten officers ran toward the hostage taker and pinned him to the ground. Three more ran toward the officer who'd been hit. Officer John Birch.

Two officers started CPR while a third applied pressure to stop the bleeding. An ambulance was called.

Chris's heartbeat escalated. He didn't know Officer Birch well, but he knew it was unlikely he'd survive until the ambulance arrived.

He also knew it could have been any one of them. It was just dumb luck he was the one to be sent to take the hostage taker into custody.

He thought about the officer on the ground. He wasn't very old; mid thirties perhaps. He felt for the man's family. His wife, his children, and even his parents. He couldn't imagine what they were about to go through. His heart was breaking for them all.

It seemed like forever until the paramedics arrived, but, it was only minutes. They began to work on the officer within seconds, but it was too late. He'd been shot through the heart and would have died almost immediately, they were told.

As the heartbreaking scene played out in front of him, Chris noticed a terrified young woman with a small child walk slowly out of the front door. She looked scared and bewildered at the scene in front of her.

He gingerly walked toward her, realizing that through the chaos that had ensued, no one else had noticed her. She was carrying the child and clinging to her tightly.

A police woman caught up to Chris, and together they helped the woman with the child and took them to the waiting ambulance.

When he had woken this morning, Chris had no idea this was how deadly the day would become.

# Chapter Two

**Charlotte watched as** her aunt made cup after cup of coffee and put them into carry trays, then placed those trays onto a trolley. She asked Charlotte to bag up at least two dozen muffins as well.

Lizzie had heard what happened and wanted to help where she could. That was so typical of her aunt.

It was only a couple of blocks to the sheriff's office, and between them they would manage the filled trolley.  It was the least they could do, Lizzie had told her, and Charlotte knew she was right.

What those poor men had been through this afternoon didn't bear thinking. She knew what her own dear Dale had endured in such circumstances.

Between them they lifted the trolley up the steps to the historical building and headed toward reception, where Lizzie was prepared to drop and run.

As they were about to leave, Chase came out of his office. Chris wasn't far behind him.

The two men looked drained.

Lizzie ran to them and hugged them both. "I was so scared when I heard." she said, hugging them again.

Charlotte had never seen her aunt so upset. "We bought coffee and muffins for the troops," she said, hoping the interruption might calm her aunt. Lizzie turned toward her and smiled.

"Of course," she said. "I was so worried I almost forgot." She laughed a bitter laugh. "That is why we're here."

Chase led them into the break room and rounded up his staff. He put his arm around Lizzie and squeezed her shoulders. "You're a good ol' bird," he told her affectionately.

Charlotte took in the scene. As a newcomer to town, she could see why her aunt had stayed here so long.

She spotted Chris and offered him a coffee. "Thanks Charlotte," he said, taking a cup of the brew. "That will really hit the spot."

Their fingers touched as she handed over the cup, and a thrill went through her. Surely that was because of the circumstances? She didn't even know this man. Barely anyway. They'd only met this morning, and that was only fleeting.

She had to admit to herself she'd taken notice of him at the store. Then she reminded herself she wasn't interested in other men. That is, other than Dale.

And certainly not another cop. She'd done her time as a cop's wife and look what happened. She'd been right to worry.

Chris put on a good façade but being married to a cop for so long she knew the signs. The dark circles under his eyes, the way he held his body, and the slight tremor in his hands.

What he'd been through today had affected him more than he would ever let on.

She passed over a muffin and he quickly took it. "You're a great cook," he told her, taking a mouthful.

She smiled at him. "Thanks," she said. "I do my best."

"Don't tell your aunt," he said conspiratorially. "But these are way better than she's ever made."

"Is that so, Christian?" Aunt Lizzie laughed as she hugged him again. "I'm so glad you boys are all okay." She stayed close to Chris and Chase, looking them both up and down.

Charlotte couldn't begin to imagine the mess she'd be in if either of them had been hurt. She moved closer to her aunt and put her arms around her, letting her know she was there for her.

She had no plans to leave any time soon, and perhaps she needed to let her aunt know that sooner rather than later. She seemed to need reassurance right now.

As the coffee and muffins ran out, the room cleared. "You're a very decent and special woman, Lizzie," Chris told her. "On behalf of us all, thank you." He gave her a long hug, then left the room.

"He's right," Charlotte said, clearing the rubbish away. "You are very special, and we all love you."

~~~

**The funeral for Officer** John Birch was well attended, not only by those who knew him, but out of respect, several officers from River Valley also attended, including Sheriff Callahan, Deputy Dolan, Officer Sawyer and more.

Lizzie also attended, Chris noted. She really was a wonderful lady, and he admired her greatly.

After the service, everyone congregated for the wake. It was a time to reflect on the life of Officer Birch.

The church had been packed, and it had been difficult to see who had attended apart from his immediate colleagues and some locals.

At the wake, Lizzie noticed a woman surrounded by the man's colleagues. As though in a protective cocoon. "It's his wife," Chris told her. "Their baby is due in just a few weeks," he added as she took in her very pregnant belly.

"And now a child grows up without its daddy." Her voice broke, and she turned her head away. Chris slid his arm around the concerned woman and pulled her close.
~~~

"It's a very sad situation," he said, looking down at the distressed woman. "But what can you do?" It was a rhetorical question, but Lizzie answered anyway after thinking for just a short time.

She spoke so quietly, Chris nearly missed it. "We can hold a fundraiser," she said. "Raise money for the child's future."

"That's a great idea," he told her. "But it will take a lot of work to organise." He squeezed her shoulder and thought that would be the end of it. Knowing Lizzie, he should have known better.

"Okay, that's settled then," she said. "I'll get a committee together and we'll make plans." Her mind made up, Lizzie gave him a hug, and whispered in his ear. "I'll let you know when the first committee meeting is being held."

Chris stared at Lizzie's back as she retreated. *What just happened?* He didn't agree to anything. Or did he?

He honestly didn't think so, but he wouldn't object. A fellow officer had died, and his wife had been left to bring up an as-yet unborn child. Her life was going to be difficult. The least they could do was make it as easy as possible.

Now all he had to do was wait for Lizzie's call and follow her orders. He grinned knowing that's exactly what he'd end up doing.

~~~

As Chris entered the café, Charlotte noticed the dark circles under his eyes.
~~~

The previous day's activities had affected everyone. Not just those directly involved, but people from surrounding areas, as well as friends of the officers involved.

Not to mention the slain officer's family.

Charlotte had not long left the kitchen when she saw him. He looked bedraggled and decidedly tired.

She stopped mid-stride.

He looked up and strode toward her, taking the heavy tray out of her hands.

"Charlotte," he said, nodding his head.

Her heart skipped a beat. *Since when did she react this way to perfect strangers?* But she knew the answer to that – since she met Deputy Christian Dolan, that's when.

Her aunt would mention him several times a day, dropping hints about the eligible bachelor, hoping it would pique her interest.

From what she'd seen so far, he was not looking for a relationship, and just quietly, neither was she.

Charlotte would happily accept his friendship. She could do with a few good friends. Moving to a new town, away from everything she loved and knew had been hard. Particularly given the circumstances.

She put her hand over his. "Christian," she said quietly. "You look tired. I, um," She gazed into his eyes. "I know yesterday was difficult. Is there anything I can do to help?"

She pulled her hand away as he moved toward the front counter and Aunt Lizzie, who was watching every move, as she often did.

He deposited the heavy tray on the back counter, ready for the two women to place the baked goods into the glass display cabinet.

"An extra-large coffee would be good," he said, reaching into his pocket. "And maybe one of those blueberry muffins."

"That's not what I meant," she snapped. She felt annoyed but knew she shouldn't. She'd seen Dale like this after a siege. It was part of the after-shock from such an event.

She snatched up the tray and started toward the kitchen. Chris was a step behind her. "Let me," he said. Reluctantly she surrendered the heavy item.

"Thanks," she said as they moved toward the kitchen. "Christian, I..."

He stared at her so intently she stopped talking. "I guess it doesn't matter," she said, putting the tray above the oven. She wanted to tell him about Dale. That she understood what he was feeling, how it affected him.

But the moment was lost.

"Well, I guess I'd best be off. Criminals to catch, paperwork to do," he said hurriedly, then tipped his hat to her.

And just like that he was gone.

Charlotte's heart sank. She felt empty, incomplete when he wasn't around. As though something was missing from her life.

She shook herself. What a crazy way to feel. The man was almost a stranger, yet she felt connected to him. Now, she wasn't sure, but there was something. Some weird sort of spark.

Perhaps they really *were* meant to be friends, and the universe was telling her so?

Charlotte heard the tinkle of the bell above the door and knew he'd left. It was time to get moving. Once the mid-morning rush started she wouldn't have time to think.

The door to the kitchen opened.

"What's going on Charlotte," Lizzie asked curiously.

Charlotte looked at her but didn't really see her. "Charlotte?"

She waved her hand across in front of her face. "Nothing aunty." When Lizzie didn't seem convinced, Charlotte reiterated. "Really, it's nothing." She turned back to preparing for the rush hour.

~~~

**Charlotte had just** finished cutting up the second carrot cake for the day and placing it in the display cabinet when she saw the police vehicle pull up out the front.

The little bell tinkled. "Afternoon, Charlotte."
~~~

The way her name rolled off his tongue made her heart sing. "Christian," she said, her heart fluttering. "What can I do for you on this gloomy afternoon."

"If you have any Cornish pasties, I'll have two of those and a large coffee. Thanks."

"To have here or takeaway?" She waved toward the sea of empty tables.

He checked his watch. "I'll have it here today," he said, then strolled toward a table close to the kitchen.

Charlotte plated his meal and placed it in front of him, then returned to make his coffee.

Lizzie came rushing in from the storage area. "I'll do that," she told Charlotte. "You need a break. Go and sit with Christian."

It was a demand, not a request. Besides, she *did* need a break. She'd been baking since early this morning. Supplies had gotten low very quickly at the mid-morning rush, and she'd had to start baking again almost immediately to ensure the upcoming lunch rush would be covered.

She sat opposite Christian and immediately breathed a sigh of relief. She didn't realise how much she'd needed a break.

"Aunty says I have to sit with you," she said with a grin. "Do you mind?"

He looked up sharply, then laughed. "I fear the old dear is trying to push us together." She looked at him in horror, and he added, "She has a habit of doing

33

that sort of thing, you know. She's a notorious match-maker."

Charlotte was shocked. She had no idea. "Does she do this often," she asked as he continued to eat.

Lizzie chose that moment to deposit two coffees on the table. One for Christian and another for Charlotte. "Enjoy, you two," she said, then returned to the front counter.

Charlotte laughed. "We were nearly sprung! So tell me, does she do it often?"

Christian took a sip of coffee, then stared at her over the brim of the mug. "Are you kidding me? Nearly every eligible bachelor in town has been partnered up and married off – all because of your dear aunt."

She sat there open mouthed. "No. Really?" She couldn't believe her laid back and generally quiet aunt would do such a thing.

Christian looked across to Lizzie. She was still at the front counter. He leaned in and Charlotte did the same. "There are still a handful of us around, but not many. Every opportunity she gets, she partners us up."

Charlotte sat there in disbelief.

Christian finished off his food and wiped his mouth with a napkin. "Now that she's decided we are to be together, she won't give up until we are." He looked at her pointedly. "You know that, right?"

She sat back in her seat. "Please tell me you are joking," she said in a whisper.

He was amused at her distress, which irritated her no end. "There's a way around it," he said, apparently brewing up an idea. "We can pretend to like each other."

She was rather taken aback at that, and also annoyed. "Well, I like *you*," she said in a huff. "Don't you like me?" She placed her arms across her chest. "As a friend," she quickly added.

He grinned. "Of course I do. But that's not what Lizzie wants. She wants us dating." He looked at her crossed arms. "Don't be mad. I'm just the messenger."

She sat there stewing for about a minute, then sipped her coffee. "Well..." Did she really want to do this? It was a big ask, but Christian did seem like a nice guy. "Okay," she said. "But I need to lay my cards on the table before we decide whether or not to do this."

He frowned at her. What did he think she was about to say?

She put both hands palm down either side of her coffee and braced herself. "I left Los Angeles because of my husband." Her voice broke and she felt her resolve dissolving.

"Your husband? You're married?" Christian's voice rose in disbelief.

"He was a cop," she said. "He..." she couldn't get the words out. "He's dead," she said quietly. "Killed on duty three years ago."

His hand slid across the table and covered hers. "I'm so sorry," he said. "And now your aunt is trying to throw us together, and you're probably not interested in another guy wearing the uniform." His expression was compassionate. "Am I right?"

She nodded, and he squeezed her hand.

"So back to our plan," he said, empathy written all over his face. *Damn! She didn't want sympathy, from him or anyone else.*

"I guess it's my turn to come clean," he said, and braced himself to do just that. "I need to say right up front I'm not interested in a relationship."

He looked down into his lap, his hand still covering hers. She stared at their entwined hands. It felt nice. Warm and comfortable, and if she was honest with herself, she didn't want him to move it.

"Christian, you don't...."

She hadn't heard her aunt move, but suddenly she was hovering over them. "Everything all right here," she asked, as though they were regular customers, and not a couple she was trying to set up.

Christian cleared his throat. "Everything is fine," he said. "More than fine in fact. I've asked Charlotte to come out with me tonight." He grinned at Charlotte who smiled.

Lizzie clapped her hands together. "Yes!" It was like a war dance, and Charlotte began to see that Christian was not being untruthful earlier. Her aunt really was trying to push them together.

"Where are you going?" She directed the question at Christian, who couldn't stop grinning.

"Uh, not sure yet," he said. "We were just working that out when you arrived." He was taking a last sip of coffee as his pager went off. "Sorry, I have to go." He pushed a notebook over to Charlotte. "Write your cell phone in here, and I'll call you later."

She scribbled her number down in disbelief that this had all unfolded so quickly, then pushed the notebook back to him.

"Sorry, gotta go." And before she knew what was happening, Christian had left the café.

~~~

**Chris got out of his** vehicle and walked toward Lizzie's "cottage" as she so fondly called it.

Charlotte stepped out of the front door.

He stepped back momentarily in surprise then circled her, looking her up and down. "Words fail me," he said, and he wasn't lying. She was the most beautiful creature he'd ever set eyes on.

She leaned forward and planted a kiss on his cheek. "You're not so bad yourself," she said, as she winked at him. "You scrub up pretty well."

He reached over and took her hand. Need to keep up the pretence for Lizzie's sake. Just as the thought entered his head, the lady herself stepped out of the cottage.

"You both look pretty snazzy," she said, giving them the once over. "What's on the agenda for tonight?"

Chris squeezed Charlotte's hand. "Dinner in Bolton, maybe at the Chinese restaurant, depending on where Charlotte would like to go, then a movie."
~~~

Lizzie smiled. She obviously wanted to see her niece happy after the tragedy she'd endured. "Wonderful," she said quietly. "Enjoy – both of you."

He held the car door while Charlotte sat down, then went to the driver's side. When he looked up again, Lizzie was gone. Probably off celebrating her match-making skills he decided as he chuckled. Little did she know.

~~~

"I had a wonderful night," Charlotte told Chris as he slowed outside Lizzie's cottage.

It was late – nearly midnight, but he didn't care. He'd had a wonderful night with Charlotte. If he didn't know better, he'd think it was a real date, not something they'd concocted to get Lizzie off their backs.

He had to admit, if she hadn't interfered with her match-making, they may have gotten together naturally. Maybe.

Or maybe not.

But this was not real. He had to keep reminding himself of that.

Nor did he want it to be real. His brother had gone to hell and back when he'd fallen in love, and Chris was not going to allow himself to be put in the same position.

"Charlotte," he said, wanting to clear the air. She'd declared her situation, and now it was time for
~~~

him to do the same. "I think it's only fair, I tell you I don't want a relationship." He took a deep breath.

"Neither do I, silly," she said, leaning across to give him a peck on the cheek. "This is all pretend, remember?" She leaned back in her seat. "For auntie's benefit."

"I have to tell you something," he said. "It's only fair, because you told me about your husband."

She stared into his eyes and lifted her hand to his shoulder. "You don't have to," she said. "There's no obligation...."

He interrupted her words. "Obligation or not, I need to say it before you hear it from someone else." He stared unblinkingly into her hazel coloured eyes and took a deep breath. "My sister-in-law killed herself and my beautiful little baby niece." He spoke so quietly, she probably wouldn't have heard if they hadn't been in the confines of his car.

"Oh my gosh!" Charlotte blurted out. "That is so horrible. You must have been devastated." He watched as tears welled in her eyes. "I mean, I was distraught about my husband's death, but a baby? That is beyond comprehension." He brushed her cheek and wiped a stray tear from her face.

Her bottom lip quivered, and he pulled her to him in a comforting hug.

"It was a long time ago," he whispered. "But it still hurts like hell."

She pulled back and gazed into his glistening eyes. "And that's why you don't want a relationship. Am I right?"

His head shot up. She knew him better than he knew himself. Until now, he had never admitted that fact. Not to anyone else, nor to himself.

"Does," she adjusted her shirt that didn't need adjusting, and wiped another tear from her cheek. "Does my aunt know?"

He laughed. "Your aunt knows everything about everyone that ever walked into this town, let alone into her café." He grinned and felt better for it. "Yeah, she knows. And she was there when I needed her. She's a wonderful person, your aunt."

"Anyway, enough of this," he said. "On a brighter note, when would you like to go out again." He brushed a stray tendril of hair behind her ear, and then realised this was the first time he'd seen her without her cook's hat on. That was why she looked so different. He gave himself an invisible head slap.

"Your hair looks beautiful, by the way," he said, trying to penetrate the depths of her eyes.

She reached up and covered his hand. "Flattery will get you everywhere." She squirmed in her seat before answering. "I have Saturday's off," she said. "So maybe next Saturday?"

She smiled and his whole world lit up. He had to remind himself again they were not dating for real.

This lady took his breath away, and he didn't know what to do about it.

~~~
~~~

# Their next *date* was a little different.

After dinner, Chris decided to take her to the lookout up on the hill. You could see all over River Valley from there. And then some.

It looked good during the day, but at night it came into itself. Amazing and beautiful. Just like Charlotte.

He winced. His thoughts went to her too much. This was all about keeping Lizzie off their backs, and nothing more. He forgot that at his peril.

The place was near deserted at this time of night. People had no idea what they were missing.

He opened the door for Charlotte and guided her to the lookout in the muted light. It was a full moon, which was just as well, since the lighting was out. No doubt the vandals had been up there again.

They were walking side by side toward the lookout when he suddenly felt compelled to touch her. His hand slid into hers and she stopped momentarily, searching his face. Then she squeezed his hand and continued on.

His heart skipped a beat. She didn't push him away, didn't force her hand out of his. His heart was happy, but he wasn't sure he was.

This was supposed to be pretend, and he was feeling things about this woman he had no intentions of feeling. Things he shouldn't be feeling when it wasn't real.

"Oh, it's beautiful!" She was standing at the protective fence; the one that stopped visitors from falling down the hillside.

He stood behind her. "Yes it is," he said, moving a little closer.

She rubbed her hands up and down her arms.

"Cold?"

"A little," she replied. "I should have brought a jacket."

He leaned forward and wrapped his arms around her in an effort to keep her warm. He knew the moment he did it, he'd made a mistake.

She felt soft and gentle. But he could feel the coolness on her skin. And that's what this was about, right? Keeping her warm.

He leaned in further, until his cheek was against her cheek. It felt nice standing here like this with Charlotte.

He closed his eyes tight. *What was he thinking?* Neither of them wanted a relationship, this was *all* for show.

Her heard her intake of breath. "It's really beautiful," she said quietly. "I've never seen anything like it. Thank you for bringing me here." She turned around in his arms and smiled.

His heart beat a little faster as he looked at her lips. Her warm and inviting lips. The lips he wanted to kiss right now.

He started to lean in, slid his hands up her arms. "Charlotte," he said. "I need to confirm this is all a ruse." He took a breath. "To get your aunt off our backs."

She stared into his eyes for longer than he'd expected. Then her tongue darted out and licked her lips. "Of course it is," she said, turning her head away. "We both said we didn't want to get involved."

He dropped his hands to his sides, and sighed, then pretended everything was okay. "Over to the left is River Valley," he said, pointing to their little town. "To the right is Hudson Falls, another tiny town."

He would keep up the pretence, they both would.

# CHAPTER THREE

"**First we eat, then** we get down to business."

Charlotte placed a meal in front of each of the committee members for the fundraiser, then one for herself. She sat next to Chris since that was the only empty seat available. He was certain Lizzie planned it that way.

The table was a little crammed, and her thigh pushed gently against his. It felt nice. Better than nice in fact. Cosy.

"This is fabulous," Chris said, glancing at Charlotte. "Where did you learn to cook?"

Lizzie stared across at him. "Charlotte," she said pointedly, "Is a trained pastry chef. Her food is amazing." She smiled across at her niece, but her glare toward him sent daggers.

"I'm not surprised," he answered, savouring every mouthful. "This is delicious."

He surveyed the roast beef on his plate. Not only did it taste delicious, it looked amazing. "Thank you," he said to both women. "I have no idea what I would have eaten tonight. Nothing as wonderful as this, that's for sure."

Charlotte blushed. "You are very welcome," she said, obviously embarrassed at the fuss. "But it's nothing. A roast is one of the easiest meals of all to make."

"It *is* very good," Sheriff Chase Callahan added. "Best I've ever had. Not that yours is bad, Lizzie," he quickly added.

Chris grinned. Lizzie was touchy about her cooking. Always had been.

"Just eat the damned food so we can get on with it," Lizzie demanded.

There was no more talk. What Lizzie demanded, Lizzie got. Most of the time.

After the dishes were cleared away, dessert was served. Strawberry cheesecake with cream on the side. While Charlotte served dessert, Lizzie made coffee for everyone.

"Right. We'll start the meeting while we eat dessert," she said putting the last of the coffees on the table. "First I'd like to thank everyone for coming, and special thanks goes to Charlotte for the delicious meal."

"Here, here." Several people spoke at once. They were all in agreement about the meal.

Chris moved his leg even closer to hers, in a personal acknowledgement. Charlotte's eyes opened wide, then she smiled at him.

"First on the agenda," Lizzie brought him out of his revelry. "Missy Callahan has offered to be the entertainment, along with her backing crew." Lizzie looked around the table. "Any objections?"

No one would object, Chris was certain. Missy was an amazing singer.

"No? Good." She scribbled something on the paper in front of her. "Next, Charlotte has offered to cook a three-course meal. The community hall has a commercial kitchen, so that won't be an issue." She looked down at the paper again. "I have included the proposed menu on the agenda. Please read it, and then we'll vote."

"Wow, amazing," Chris said, reading the list of food. "I'm definitely going to this," he said, licking his lips.

Lizzie laughed. "You're going anyway. You're on the committee, remember?"

Chris felt the heat move up his face. *What was he thinking?*

When Charlotte was around he didn't think, couldn't think. She was getting inside his head, which was not part of the plan.

He had always been so level-headed, a clear-thinker. His own person. Now he was tongue-tied where Charlotte was concerned, and it had to stop.

Chase laughed out loud. "Good one, Chris," he said.

As they worked their way through the agenda, and everything on Lizzie's list, his mind was on the woman sitting next to him.

He stared at her profile. She was the most beautiful woman he'd ever seen.

Suddenly she turned and glanced at him. *Had she seen him staring?* His heart sped up, and he wondered what it would be like to hold her in his arms.

~~~

**After all the planning** the fundraising committee – meaning Lizzie, Charlotte, and Chris and a few others – had done over the past few weeks, the day had finally arrived.

They'd decided on a dinner dance arrangement, but there was to be a number of charity auctions throughout the night.

Most of the locals had turned up for the event, along with locals from the slain officer's county. They should raise quite a bit of money for his family, which was the whole point of the fundraiser.

Chris stood at the door, greeting people as they arrived, resplendent in his police uniform. They'd decided that out of respect for the slain officer, all police personal would attend the evening in full uniform.
~~~

He stood there, hopefully looking smart, greeting the guests, and directing them to their tables. He also had to mingle with the crowd after everyone had arrived. He had it easy.

He looked across the room to where Lizzie was rushing about, Charlotte by her side.

The pair were setting up the tables ready for the silent auction lists, which would be brought out later.

There was to be a sit-down dinner with three courses. Alcohol was not included, and that would be another source of revenue for the night.

But the main source, at least they hoped, would be from the auctions that were to be held throughout the evening.

Lizzie was giving away five dinner-for-two vouchers, the local boutique gave two one-hundred-dollar vouchers to spend at their store, plus several notable donations from other local businesses, including The Bar and Grill where Chase's sister-in-law Missy used to work – before she'd had her baby, his precious niece.

Chris tipped his hat as Charlotte glanced across at him. Their eyes met, and he couldn't pull himself away from her. She had some sort of pull on him, and Chris desperately tried to free himself.

It didn't work.

It wasn't until Lizzie touched Charlotte on the arm, needing her help, that the trance she'd put him in ended.

He shook himself. This was crazy. He didn't react to women like this.

He wasn't interested in women. Any women. After what happened to his brother, he'd sworn off them years ago.

But Charlotte was different. He had feelings for her – she was a wonderful person, and someone he'd like to spend more time with. He couldn't deny it.

"Hello Chris." It was Mrs Simpson, who he'd known most of his life. She was a lovely lady and could always be relied on for support.

He moved into hug the woman who had been a constant in his life. Even through the tragedy. "Hello Mrs Simpson. Good to see you," he said as he moved out of her embrace. He checked the table list and directed her accordingly. "We'll catch up later," he said, and meant it.

Soft music began to play, which was a cue for people to take their places at the tables.

Chase had agreed to be the MC for the night, and stood on the stage, holding a microphone.

"Good evening ladies and gentlemen," he said, looking around. He waited a few moments while people finished taking their seats. "Thank you all for coming. Despite the tragedy that has brought us together, the death of a local officer, we hope you enjoy your evening."

He referred to papers he held in his hands. "Your meal tonight has been provided by Aunt Lizzie's Kitchen. Prepared by Lizzie's niece, Charlotte Jones." He took a breath. "I know she doesn't want the accolades, but the entire meal tonight has been donated by Aunt Lizzie's Kitchen."

The audience applauded and whistled. "First course will be delivered to you shortly," he added. Then walked off the stage.

The music continued as people talked amongst themselves.

Everyone had now arrived, and Chris moved toward the committee table, acknowledging people as he made his way there.

Each place setting also had a list of the night's auctions. Chris hoped it would bring in a huge amount of cash for Officer John Birch's widow. It was the very least they could do for a colleague.

"How much do you think you'll bring in, Chris?" The question came out of the blue. "No idea Mrs Simpson. We'll have several lines of revenue, so it's hard to say."

She grinned. "No. I mean how much do you think *you* will bring in!"

Chris frowned, not understanding the question. "Christian, Christian," Lizzie called across the room. "I need your help please."

He made his way across to the agitated woman, as the music got a little louder. "I need help to move this table in place," she said. "We'll hold the auctions between each course."

They'd just finished putting everything in place when Chase took to the stage again.

"Entrée will be served shortly," he said. "Please take your place at the tables."

Charlotte had already prepared the entrée dishes, which would be served to the guests shortly. With help from Lizzie, she had already begun work on the main course.

This was not a night off for either of them.

"Aunty," Chris heard Charlotte say. "Why don't you sit down and have entrée? I will be fine."

Lizzie looked at her quizzically. "You're cooking for a lot of people," she said, sounding exasperated.

"I do have some kitchen hands," Charlotte said, equally exasperated. "You should take a break. I promise I'll let you know if I need you."

Chris led Lizzie to the committee table and made sure she rested. He poured her a glass of wine, and sat down next to her, relieved to be finally sitting down himself.

The entrées came out a few minutes later. Alternate honey mustard chicken wings and vegie-stuffed mushrooms.

The food was amazing, but Chris felt guilty, knowing Charlotte was in the kitchen slaving away to produce such a magnificent spread.

"And now for a little entertainment." Chase's voice rang out over the loud speaker system. "Our very own Missy Callahan has agreed to perform for us tonight."

He waited patiently while the crowd whistled and applauded. "Just give us a few minutes to get her set up, and then we'll get to hear the voice of an angel."

Missy stood at her table, passing baby Chloe over to her father, Rory, then scampered out the back to get into her costume.

It hadn't been that long since little Chloe was born, so Chris had been surprised when Missy had offered to perform. She was such a trooper in his book.

Chris helped with the setting up. The musicians from The Bar and Grill, where she performed before giving birth, had volunteered their time, so were there to back her up. Such a giving community.

Once the electric keyboard was ready to go, Missy stepped out onto the stage to a huge applause.

She bowed to the crowd, then indicated for the music to start.

She began singing *I Want to be a Cowboy's Sweetheart,* her most requested song. And from what Chris could gather, a personal favourite. She looked across at Rory and winked.

Rory held the baby up so Missy could see her and whispered in the baby's ear. No doubt it was something like "That's your mommy singing."

The fact she'd become a cowboy's sweetheart was quite ironic.

When she finished, the audience exploded. Missy bowed to them, then indicated to the musicians to begin another song. It was accepted equally as well.

When she finished, Missy bowed again, then indicated for the crowd to acknowledge her musicians, as she always did.

"That's is for now, Y'all," she said. "Don't go away, I'll be back later." Meeting her at the stage steps with baby Chloe, Rory kissed his wife and hugged her, with the baby in his arms.

Chris watched every movement, and his throat became tight.

*What would it be like to have a family of his own?* The tragedy that his brother endured was unthinkable. Chris had long decided he couldn't put himself through something like that.

Chase's voice came over the loud speaker again. "Isn't she magnificent? We are so blessed to have such a talented lady in our midst. Please thank the amazing Missy Callahan!" He stood and waited until the applause died down, then made another announcement. "Main course will be served shortly. Don't go away."

He began to leave the stage, then doubled back. "I almost forgot," he said. "The first group of auctions will begin in just a few minutes. Then we'll eat, and there will be more auctions after main course."

He turned off the microphone and placed it on a table, then walked over to Aunt Lizzie and whispered in her ear.

Chris watched the exchange carefully. *What the heck were they up to?*

Lizzie grabbed some cards from the table Chris had helped set up, then went on stage. "The first auction of the night is for a dinner for two at Aunt Lizzie's Kitchen," she said. "I have five vouchers available and will auction them off separately."

"All auctions tonight will be run as silent auctions, so I will tell you the items available, then you go over to the table," she pointed in the general direction, "and write down your bid."

No one moved. "You have twenty minutes," she said, looking around the room. "So get your skates on!"

People stood, chairs were scraped backwards, and couples talked between themselves. Suddenly the table was a frenzy of activity, and Lizzie smiled.

She took her place at the table again and whispered to Chris. "It's looking good. Lots of bids equals lots of money for Officer Birch's family."

They chatted between themselves for the next twenty minutes, then Lizzie took to the stage again. "Thanks everyone. Time is *up*. Winners will be announced later this evening."

Chase went on to the stage and took the microphone from Lizzie. "Main course is about to be served. Please take your place at the tables."

Waitresses began to pour out of the kitchen to serve the guests who were eagerly awaiting their meals.

Main course was put in front of Chris and was smoked salmon with a side salad. The alternative was roast chicken with gravy and roasted vegetables. They both looked delicious. Charlotte had certainly outdone herself tonight.

There was low chatter amongst the guests, and soft music played in the background. The food was beyond all expectations, and everyone certainly seemed to be enjoying it. Chris definitely was.

He felt bad that Charlotte was stuck in the kitchen while he was out here enjoying the food she'd slaved over. But, he reminded himself, they each had a job to do, a task they'd volunteered for, and this was what she chose.

He was mighty glad she did.

Charlotte was a fantastic cook, and a fabulous person. He'd enjoyed getting to know her over the past months. He liked her. A lot.

He welcomed the interruption to his wayward thoughts when Lizzie took to the microphone. He hadn't noticed her leave.

"I'd like to take this opportunity to thank you all again for coming along tonight," she said, glancing around the room. "As much as we don't want to think about it, this *is* about supporting Officer John Birch's family." She took a deep breath before speaking again.

"We will continue with the silent auctions while the tables are cleared." She rifled through some papers. "Next will be auctioning the one-hundred-dollar vouchers to the River Valley Boutique. This is a great prize, ladies," she added. She went on to list several other prizes, which would run concurrently. "Again, go to the table and bid for the prize you would like. You have twenty minutes, and then I will announce another auction item."

He couldn't fathom why, but Lizzie winked at him. Chris tried to remember what all the donated prizes had been. Nothing untoward as far as he could recall. He shrugged his shoulders and took a sip of the iced water sitting in front of him.

Mrs Simpson walked over on her way to the auction table and tapped him on the shoulder. "This is so exciting," she said, then leaned forward and whispered in his ear. "I've heard there's a secret prize on auction. Do you know what it is?" she asked, a twinkle in her eye and a smile on her lips.

He frowned. *A secret prize? Not that he'd heard of, but with Lizzie you never could tell.*

The soft music started again, Mrs Simpson wandered away to talk to a few other guests. Chris got up from the table and started to mingle.

"You look very nice," he heard one elderly lady say, right before she ran her hand up his muscled arms. He smiled and walked away. What was it with women and uniforms?

After doing his mingling duty, Chris made his way back to his seat as he noticed Lizzie heading toward the stage.

Chase was already there. "Once all the auctions are finished up, dessert will be served," he said, then handed the microphone to Lizzie.

"Can I have everyone's attention," she said, then waited for the chatter to die down. "We have a last-minute auction prize." She smiled at Chris then nodded her head. "For those who are not aware, there will be an opportunity for dancing later in the evening. This prize is one you won't see often. You could say it's unique, as it will probably never happen again." People began to chatter, speculating what it could be.

This was obviously what Mrs Simpson was talking about. But he was still none the wiser.

Lizzie turned toward him, and his heart began to pound. "Deputy. Christian Dolan, would you please stand," she said, determination on her face.

"Deputy Dolan has kindly offered to be dance partner for not one, but two lucky ladies tonight." The crowd began to applaud and whistle, and Chris looked around, confused.

"Wha...." He didn't offer this. *What the hell was going on?* Then he realized. That crafty Lizzie. She was always up to something. It was too late to back out. He'd look like a fool if he did that, so he'd go along with it.

"Bid sheets are on the table, ladies." She began to walk away. "Or gentlemen," she laughed, then backed off.

Chris made his way toward the stage. "You cheeky thing," he whispered in her ear when he got close. "I didn't offer that." He was only slightly annoyed. It was for a good cause, after all.

Lizzie patted him on the back. "Now, now," she said. "Don't fret. You might end up with a stunning young lady." She grinned then scurried away.

"Once again, we have the amazing Missy Callahan," Chase announced, then handed the microphone to Missy.

The music began, and she started singing *Crazy*. A song made famous by Patsy Cline. The audience applauded loudly, and the noise was almost overwhelming.

Chris was amazed to see baby Chloe was sound asleep in her father's arms. Rory rocked the baby while his wife sang her heart out.

She bowed as she finished singing, and once again acknowledged the musicians. "I'll be back shortly," she said. "I believe there will be another announcement first." She grinned, then handed the microphone to Chase, her brother-in-law.

"If we could have a little bit of hush," he said, "I will announce the winners of the silent auctions." He shuffled through the papers and found what he was looking for. "For the dinner for two at Aunt Lizzie's Kitchen - there are five winners, and they are..."

He read out five sets of names. "See me at the end of the night to make payment and get your vouchers. Chase went on to read out all the remaining winners. "Thank you all very much for your generosity," he said.

"Now for the one you've all been waiting for. A dance with Deputy Chris Dolan." He grinned at his deputy, who was feeling quite queasy at this point.

"First winner is – Mrs Santini. Congratulations!" he said, nodding to the 76-year-old. Chris breathed a sign of relief. So far Lizzie's plan was not working. "Second winner is – Aunt Lizzie!" He grinned. "Congratulations Lizzie."

"And for those who want to know, that prize yielded almost one thousand dollars," he said. "Our deputy is apparently very popular with the ladies."

Chris felt the heat rise from his neck, all the way up his face. He slunk down in his chair in embarrassment. Both prize winners were way out of his age range. On reflection, he decided it was probably a good thing.

Missy took to the stage again, and the music began. As she sang Blue Moon of Kentucky, Chris went over and invited Mrs Santini to dance, and they walked out onto the dance floor.

People began to clap.

He wasn't the best dancer in town, but he also wasn't the worst. He held the older lady away from himself, but she pushed forward, until she was so close, there was no way for Chris to distance himself.

*Ah well, it was only for a few minutes and he'd be done.*

When the music ended, he accompanied the older lady back to her chair. "Thank you, Mrs Santini," he said, and started to walk away.

"No so fast, young man," she said, grabbing his arm. "I paid a lot of money to dance with you. I think I should at least get a kiss."

Chris balked, but she leaned forward and gave him a friendly peck on the cheek, then hugged him. "Now I have my money's worth," she said, laughing.

Chris sighed in relief. *What did he think? That she would kiss him on the lips? He couldn't bare to think about it.*

"Dessert is about to be served." Chase's voice came over the loud speaker, and people began to return to their tables.

Lizzie hustled out to the kitchen, meaning Chris didn't get the opportunity to talk to her about 'his offer'. She really could be sneaky at times, but since it was for a good cause, he'd let her off this time.

The waitresses began to pour out of the kitchen again, this time carrying desserts.

At least Charlotte didn't have to slave over a hot oven for the desserts. Chris knew they'd been prepared at the café.

Traditional Black Forest Cake with cream on the side, and Banana Pudding with Vanilla Wafer Crumble for the alternative. Yummy!

Chris patted his belly. He had over indulged tonight, but he didn't care. He didn't do it often, and Charlotte was an amazing chef.

And... it was for a great cause.

Just like the dance he had to have. He sighed.

At least it was Lizzie and not some bachelorette trying to tie him down. That's what usually happened at these things.

He thought back to the last dinner dance he'd attended and felt ill. The young lady in question virtually forced herself on him. Luckily, they were in a public place with lots of people around. He wasn't sure what would have happened if they'd been alone.

Dessert was over, and coffee was being served. Little Chloe was letting her presence known now that she was awake and hungry. Missy took her bottle out to the kitchen to warm up, while Rory pacified the little one by walking around with her on his shoulder.

For a tiny moment, Chris wished for his own little family. All the Callahan Brothers had now settled down, making him somewhat envious.

He shook himself. *What was he thinking? Those kinds of thoughts could only lead to disaster.*

The crying stopped when Rory put the teat of the bottle in the baby's mouth. She'd been good all night, and he couldn't deny she was a beautifully behaved little girl.

He took a sip of his coffee, watching Rory with his little treasure. He seemed so happy. Happier than he'd ever been.

Maybe...

*No!* He couldn't risk being hurt like his brother. What a terrible tragedy that turned out to be.

Now that dessert was over and baby Chloe was settled, Missy headed back to the stage, and the musical introduction began.

Chris tapped Lizzie on the shoulder, and she stood. As he accompanied her to the dance floor, she stumbled, hurting her ankle.

Charlotte, who was now out of the kitchen, ran to her aunt. She squatted down and checked the ankle.

"Oh dear," she said. "I guess you have to miss your dance with Christian now."

"Not on your Nellie!" she said, agitated. "I paid a lot of money for that dance. You'll have to take my place."

Charlotte stared at her. Chris was certain he saw the beginning of a grin on Lizzie's face, but it disappeared as quickly as it had appeared.

Charlotte hesitated momentarily, but Chris took her hand. He was becoming more and more affected by Charlotte's presence.

As he walked her to the dance floor, he felt all eyes on them.

They stood in the middle of the dance floor waiting for the music to begin, and he was sure Charlotte would be feeling as awkward as he was.

He stared into her eyes and got lost in them. He couldn't look away, he just couldn't. *Why did he feel so drawn to her?*

He felt Lizzie's eyes burn a hole in his back as he just stood there, so placed his arms around Charlotte, ready for the music.

He kept her at a distance, knowing how many pairs of eyes would be on them at this moment. They were the only couple on the dance floor at this time, but hopefully other couples would join them soon.

Chris shuffled his feet feeling a bit like a fox in a hen house – very out of place. Charlotte's arm crept up around his back, and he held her other hand.

He felt warmth trickle up his arm as Missy began to sing *I Just Died in Your Arms Tonight.*

Was someone trying to tell them something?

They danced their way around the dance floor. Or should he say shuffled? He was never a brilliant dancer, and with everyone watching them, he felt even more self-conscious than usual.

Charlotte looked up into his eyes. "Don't worry about them, Christian," she told him. "This is about us." She gave him a tentative smile and he remembered she'd been forced into this too.

He nodded as he thought how his name rolled off her tongue. It sounded good. He could listen to her say it all day.

Charlotte looked around the room. "No one is watching us now," she whispered as other couples joined them. "Let's just relax and enjoy ourselves."

But Chris wasn't sure he wanted to relax. If he did that, he might feel things he didn't want to feel. He might enjoy spending his time with Charlotte, and he didn't want to do that either.

Not that he didn't like her. He was enjoying their faux dates, and the times they spent together, even if it was for all the wrong reasons.

Despite himself, his arms reached around her, and unexpectedly she leaned into him. She moved slightly and rested her head against his shoulder.

It felt right. It felt good. He pulled her a little closer as they swayed to the music.

He no longer thought about the people around them. All he thought about was Charlotte. About how good she felt. About how nice it would be to kiss her right now.

His fingers slid slowly up her arm and onto her cheek. A tiny teasing smile crept into her mouth. His heart skipped a beat.

"This is nice, Christian," she said quietly, relaxing into him even more than before.

He caressed her cheek without even thinking. Hadn't realized what he was doing until it was too late. "Charlotte." His voice was equally as quiet. "I really like holding you like this," he said after long moments.

"I like it too."

Before he could think about what he was doing, he leaned down and brushed his lips against hers, ever so lightly.

He wondered exactly where it might lead.

<div align="center">~~~</div>

# Charlotte looked up.

Christian was moving closer toward her. Surely he wasn't going to... Not here, not with everyone around?

But he did.

As he gradually moved in for the kiss, she had two choices. She could back off and avoid him, or she could stay right where she was and let his lips connect with hers.

Right up until those last few seconds she hadn't decided. But his mouth looked delicious. Inviting.

So she let him kiss her.

It was a mere brushing of lips. Not a *real* kiss, but a promise of things to come maybe?

He lifted his head again, and she saw a smile on his face. Her hand went up and brushed his cheek. It was smooth and clean shaven.

Just how she liked it.

Not that she objected to a five o'clock shadow. That could be pretty sexy in itself. But she liked the way he took care of himself, even though it was him alone, with no partner.

As the music stopped she felt disappointed. She would have to let go. To lose her grip on him.

She already knew she would feel emptiness. It had been such a long time since a man had held her in his arms like this.

Heck, it seemed like forever since a man had held her at all.

She liked the way it felt. Comforting. Loving. Wonderful.

As Christian stepped away from her, she felt bereft. She didn't want him to leave, but the music had stopped. They had to return to their seats.

As they began to walk away, the music commenced again. The words of Unchained Melody rang throughout the room.

"Shall we?" Christian asked softly. And she nodded.

She could think of nothing better than being in his arms again. Being held as though nothing or no one mattered as much as she did. Right in this moment of time.

Charlotte sank into him; her arm went up his back as he held her hand. "Charlotte," he said just above a whisper. "I think I'm falling for you."

He looked down at her and her eyes opened wide. Then she winced.

She couldn't bring herself to commit to another man. Dale was the love of her life. And now he was gone.

But he wouldn't want her to stop living, she knew that for certain.

She opened her eyes again. "I,"

He put his fingers to her lips. "Shhh," he said. "You don't have to say anything. Let's just enjoy the moment."

They barely danced. It was more like a tiny shuffle across the dance floor. Other couples were dancing too, and they didn't feel like they were on display.

She closed her eyes and melted into his body. This felt so right. He felt so real.

A tear slid down her cheek.

*What about Dale? What about her dead husband?* Was it time to move on, to move forward with her life?

That was a decision only she could make. All the memories they'd made together, the plans, the children they'd wanted. Was she expected to forget it all? To just move ahead with another man, with Christian, as though none of it had happened?

She wasn't sure she was ready for any of it.

Charlotte felt him brush her tears away. "It's okay, Charlotte, I'm not asking for a life-long commitment," he said, and she felt relief.

Then he leaned down and kissed her gently. And this time she kissed him back.

# CHAPTER FOUR

**"He's a really nice bloke,"** Lizzie told Charlotte, as she packed the cooled baked goods into the glass display cabinet.

It was nearly time for the mid-morning rush, and they needed to be ready. Not that it was anything new to Lizzie. She'd run her *little coffee shop*, as she called it, for over thirty years.

She knew every person in the tiny town of River Valley and knew every eligible bachelor. She'd even tried to match some of them up with equally eligible young women.

In some cases, she'd even succeeded.

Christian and Charlotte were her current challenge, and things were coming along nicely.

She smiled at the thought.

"I'm not sure I'm *that* interested," Charlotte shot back, but Lizzie knew that wasn't true.

There was a special spark between them. It was more than obvious at the fundraiser.

Lizzie had watched them as they danced. She had set that up very nicely, if she did say so herself. It was funny how her ankle seemed fine just after they'd finished dancing.

They were meant to be together. She knew it, and Charlotte knew it.

Heck, maybe even Christian knew it.

She looked across at Charlotte and raised her eyebrows. "Charlotte...."

Her niece glared at her. "Aunty," she rounded.

Lizzie sighed. "It's been three years, Charlotte." How did you say this without upsetting her? "It's time to move on."

Charlotte's head went up sharply. "Move on?" Her voice was high pitched and got higher the longer she spoke. "Do you really think I can move on?" She shook her head. "We were soulmates," she said quietly. "We had plans. We were going to have kids." She swiped at her cheeks. "I wish we hadn't waited...."

Charlotte pulled out a chair and sat down. Lizzie sat next to her and took her hand. "I know darling. I'm sure you miss him. A lot. But Dale wouldn't want you to waste the rest of your life grieving over him." Lizzie took a deep breath. "He was a good man and he loved you. He'd want you to be happy."

Charlotte looked at her aunt, tears brimming in her eyes. "I know," she said quietly. "I just can't. Not yet. Christian knows that." She took a calming breath. "We've talked about it."

The little bell over the door tinkled and a group of workers rushed in. Charlotte stood abruptly, then rushed out the back to the kitchen. Mid-morning rush had started.

Lizzie watched her go.

Charlotte and Christian were meant to be a couple. She saw it every time they were together. There was a certain chemistry.

It wasn't her imagination, she was certain it wasn't. After all, she was pretty good at this match-making stuff.

~~~

**"Christian." Lizzie was** on the phone, calling the Sheriff's office.

"There is a group of ruffians here who are hell-bent on destroying the place." She paused for moment, then continued. "One of them is manhandling Charlotte." She listened for his response, knowing he'd rush to get there now, then hung up the phone.

It was mid-afternoon, and the café was quiet, but it was rather disturbing for the two women who were there alone.

Charlotte breathed a sigh of relief when Christian, Officer Sawyer, Officer Wrangler, and Officer Drury all strode through the door just a few minutes later, the lights and sirens on their cars still going.
~~~

River Valley might be small, but they did not skimp when it came to law enforcement.

"Afternoon gents," Deputy Christian Dolan said, as the four lawmen surrounded the table, and therefore those causing the ruckus.

Charlotte watched, horrified, as the biggest of the group made a run for it. Christian bolted after him and a fight ensued.

His hat flew across the room and Charlotte heard fabric rip. As they rolled along the floor, she noticed his shirt was the worse for wear. But that was the least of his problems.

The other two men sat quietly at the table, watching the drama unfold, the three remaining officers surrounding them. It seemed to be getting out of hand when Jason Sawyer pulled his gun. "That's enough," he yelled. "Stop where you are and put your hands in the air."

The man did not move a muscle.

Charlotte was shaking and muffled a cry when she saw the blood dripping from Christian's mouth. He reached behind him and pulled out his handcuffs, securing the man as he sat on the floor.

The deputy surveyed the chaos around the room. Chairs were strewn everywhere, and tables overturned.

"Don't worry about those," Lizzie told him. "I was more concerned about Charlotte being hurt."

As the other officers took the three men into custody, he walked over to the women. "I have to do some paperwork," he said. "Can you spare a moment or two to sit with me later?"

They nodded, and he said he would return shortly, after "sorting these three out".

Charlotte was quite shaken by the whole situation and was slumped at one of the tables when Christian returned. She heard the little bell tinkle, and knew it was him before she even turned her head.

She seemed to have a radar for him these days.

As she looked up, she saw Christian was not alone. Given their couple status, if you could call it that, she was not surprised.

Officer Jason Sawyer held a clipboard with several pages. He sat and settled himself as Christian seated himself next to Charlotte, pulling his chair as close to her as possible.

Lizzie deposited four coffees on the table, then sat next to Officer Sawyer.

"Christian," Charlotte said, worry in her voice. "Are you alright? I mean, your mouth is bleeding." He swiped at his mouth with his ripped sleeve and stared at it.

"Everyone calls me Chris," he said, totally ignoring her question about his injury. "But I like the way you say my name, so feel free to keep saying it."

Officer Sawyer's head shot up, but Chris chose to ignore him. He grinned at her, then winked, and she felt relieved, but embarrassed at his public declaration.

He might have taken a battering, but his ego hadn't.

As he took a sip of coffee, he shuffled the paperwork in front of the other officer. "Sorry, but we have to do this," he said taking her hand.

He nodded at the officer sitting across from him and Jason began. "So, let's start at the beginning," he said.

Charlotte lifted her coffee to her lips. The sweet beverage slid down her throat and she felt somewhat comforted. What happened today would stay with her a long time.

"The bastards stormed into the café and tore the place apart," Lizzie said, annoyance in her voice.

Charlotte nearly spat out her coffee.

Christian and Jason both laughed, but she took a deep breath, and then another sip of coffee. They were patient and waited until she was ready.

"I'd just finished putting the baked goods into the glass display cabinet when they came in. As I walked back to the kitchen, the big one grabbed my hand." She took another breath, and another sip of coffee.

Chris reached out and covered her hand with his. "Did he hurt you," he asked quietly. "Because if he did..."

"He didn't hurt me," she said quickly, trying to dissipate the anger he was barely controlling. "He grabbed me and pulled me into a bear hug." She looked down into the coffee that she barely saw. "I pulled away, and that's when he got angry."

Christian's face darkened with fury.

"Then what happened?" he asked, despite Jason being in control of this interview.

But he kept his hand right where it was, covering hers.

Charlotte glanced at their intertwined hands, she didn't dare look at him in case she broke down.

"He, he threw a chair across the room," she said, barely controlling her emotions. "I was really scared. For myself and aunty," she said, close to tears.

Jason scribbled her answers as she spoke.

Christian's head shot up. With any other victim he would just ignore the emotion. She knew he would. But she wasn't any other victim.

He'd held her in his arms. He'd kissed her. He'd told her he was falling for her.

There was an emotional connection between them. There was that indefinable something there.

She looked into his face, and his expression changed. It went from anger to compassion in a flash.

He suddenly stood, scraping the chair behind him. He pulled her up from where she sat and enveloped her in the biggest hug she could ever remember receiving.

She cried quietly against his chest. He just stood there and let her.

Charlotte heard Lizzie shift in her seat. Now she sat back and stared at them. A smile on her face.

~~~

# Chris whistled as he strolled to Aunt Lizzie's Kitchen.

It was official now; he and Charlotte were a couple. And he didn't care who knew about it.

Despite the ruse they'd carried out for months, just to keep Lizzie off their backs, they'd grown closer and eventually admitted they were meant for each other.

The little bell tinkled as he strolled in.

"Good Morning, Christian," Lizzie said. "The usual?"

He'd been coming for coffee every morning for some weeks now, hoping to steal some time, even a few moments, with Charlotte.

"Thanks, yes," he said, craning his neck trying to see his girl.

Lizzie grinned. "Oh, for goodness sakes," she said. "Go out to the kitchen and give her a good morning kiss!"

He was on his way when she struggled out the door with a huge tray full of steaming hot baked goods. He bolted to take it from her.

Her whole face lit up when she spotted him. "Christian," she said, breathlessly.
~~~

"Charlotte," he said nodding, and his heart skipped a beat at the sight of her. He carried the tray and placed it where the two women could fill the display cabinet.

She sat at one of the café tables, and he sat down with her. He heard the coffee machine in the background as he covered her hand.

"What wonderful creations do you recommend today," he asked, grinning like an idiot.

She looked disappointed. "Is that all you're interested in," she asked. "I thought you'd come to see me."

He laughed out loud. "I did," he whispered. "I always come to see you, but don't tell your aunt. She'd probably kick my butt." He leaned forward and gave her a peck on the cheek, staying longer than he should, reluctant to pull away.

As he pulled back, she said, "Blueberry muffins," and began to stand. "Sorry, but I have to go."

He was disappointed, but knew he'd only get to steal a few minutes of her time. The mid-morning rush wasn't far off, and she'd have plenty to do in preparation.

"Coffee's ready," Lizzie shouted across to him. She bagged up a muffin for him, and he handed across some money. As she usually did these days, Lizzie waved his money away. But as he always did, he threw it on the counter and rushed out the door.

Tonight was to be very special. He would come back later and make plans with Charlotte. After the lunch-time rush. At least then she'd be able to sit down with him and talk. He'd made it a habit to have lunch with her most days, so they got to spend as much time together as possible. When he wasn't out on a job that was.

She knew the drill. She'd lived through it with her husband.

He winced. He didn't want to think about Charlotte with anyone else. He knew that was selfish, and even a bit stupid, but he wanted to think about her as his girl. Now more than ever.

~~~

**It had become one of** their most favorite places to visit.

The food was good, but it certainly wasn't the best he'd ever eaten. Most likely, Chris decided, it was because of the muted lights, the soft music, and the intimate dance floor.

Neither of them was the greatest of dancers, but they enjoyed being in each other's arms, and just swaying to the beat.

If it hadn't been for the fundraiser, they would never have known. Neither would they have *really* gotten to know each other.

To know that despite their resistance, the universe had thrown them together for a reason. That they'd both suffered tragedy, and both needed healing.

Chris contemplated all this as he held Charlotte lovingly in his arms. Felt the deep connection they had, and never wanted it to end.
~~~

He looked down into her face, into the depths of her beautiful hazel eyes. His life had changed so completely over the past months, and despite his resolve, he had opened his heart to the wonderful woman standing here, wrapped in his arms.

His heart raced, and his head swam. What did he do to deserve such an angel?

Her eyes were closed, and she was being swept away by the music. Her face was so serene, and she looked so content. He loved the way she looked when she was happy.

Charlotte's head leaned against his chest, and he stroked her cheek as she looked up into his eyes. Did she see the love, as he saw in hers? He hoped so.

His love for her had grown immensely since he'd first held her. That was a turning point for him, and he praised God for sending her to him.

He leaned into her and kissed her mouth, and she closed her eyes. Her arms went up and stroked his back. He loved being with her, and just holding her. There was nothing he enjoyed more.

"Charlotte," he said.

She opened her eyes and looked to him. "Mmmmm?"

"I love you, Charlotte," he said so only she could hear, meaning every word.

She smiled sweetly. "I love you too."

He suddenly pulled out of her arms and dropped to his knees in the middle of the dance floor.

"Marry me, Charlotte," he said, as he pulled a ring box out of his pocket.

The other couples stopped dancing around them and began to stare, hanging on every word. But he wasn't deterred. She didn't answer, so he pulled the engagement ring out of the box and slid it on her finger. "Marry me," he said again, his heart now racing so much he wasn't sure he'd be able to stand again.

She stared at the ring, and then at Chris. He couldn't read her expression, and for a moment, he was certain she was going to say no. His heart felt like it was breaking into a million pieces.

He closed his eyes. He didn't want to see her face when she said no.

"Christian," she said, touching his cheek. "Did you hear me? I said yes!"

Everyone around them began to clap, and everything seemed to move in slow motion. He got to his feet and wrapped his arms around the love of his life. His soulmate. The woman he was going to marry.

~~~

# The wedding was a small affair.

Originally, out of respect for Charlotte and the circumstances of her husband's death, Chris thought a registry office wedding would suit Charlotte better.

But she was having none of it. So, a small chapel wedding it was.

She looked incredibly beautiful in her knee-length soft mauve gown and matching shoes. They
~~~

wanted to keep it intimate, inviting only people who were special to them, so it was close friends, family, and police family only.

As they were pronounced man and wife, Chris took his new bride by the hand and pulled her toward the chapel entrance, stopping momentarily to kiss her.

He didn't care who saw them, they were married now.

"Hello Mrs Dolan," he said, and she grinned at him.

She put a finger to her mouth. "Hmmm," she said. "Charlotte Dolan. Kinda rolls off the tongue, doesn't it?"

He hugged her tightly and didn't ever want to let her go.

The last thing he saw as they left the church was Lizzie standing at the back of the chapel, wiping tears from her face as she grinned at him.


THE END

Thank you so much for reading my book – I hope you enjoyed it.

I would greatly appreciate you leaving a review on Amazon, even if it is only a one-liner. It helps to have my books more visible on Amazon!


~~~

*To see all the books in this series visit here:*

*https://www.amazon.com/gp/product/B07DYG7SRB*


*The **River Valley Lawmen Series** is a spin-off from the popular Callahan Brothers Series.*


*To Check Out the Callahan Brothers Series, visit here:*

*https://www.amazon.com/gp/product/B078W9YCP5? ref=series_rw_dp_labf*


*All my books can be seen on my Amazon Author Page:*

*https://www.amazon.com/Cheryl- Wright/e/B0088GDSKM*
~~~

# About the Author

Multi-published, best selling and award-winning author, Cheryl Wright, former secretary, debt collector, account manager, writing coach, and shopping tour hostess, loves reading.

She writes both contemporary and historical western romance, as well as contemporary romance and romantic suspense.

She lives in Melbourne, Australia, and is married with two adult children and has six grandchildren.

When she's not writing, she can be found in her craft room making greeting cards.

Check out Cheryl's Amazon page - *https://www.amazon.com/Cheryl-Wright/e/B0088GDSKM* for a full list of her other books.

Join my Facebook Reader Group
https://www.facebook.com/groups/cherylwrightaut
hor/

Join my newsletter here!
https://mailchi.mp/534bd8eff145/cherylwright

Visit my Website
http://www.cheryl-wright.com/

www.ingramcontent.com/pod-product-compliance
Lightning Source LLC
Chambersburg PA
CBHW071542100726
47908CB00004B/1477